HURRICANES

HURRICANES

PETER MURRAY

THE CHILD'S WORLD®

It is a hot, sunny August day in South Florida. In the cold vacuum of outer space, a weather satellite detects a strange cloud over the Atlantic Ocean. The clouds are spiraling around one another, forming an enormous pinwheel hundreds of miles across. The satellite takes photographs and transmits them to the National Hurricane Center in Florida.

As soon as the weather scientists, called *meteorologists*, see the pictures, they give the area of swirling clouds a name.

They call it Tropical Storm Andrew.

The storm is hundreds of miles out to sea, still too far for weather radar to detect. But satellite photos show that it is moving toward the United States. An Air Force Hurricane Hunter plane flies out for a closer look at the approaching storm. The airplane is designed to fly in the roughest weather. Even so, the trip is dangerous. The Hurricane Hunter flies directly into the clouds. Instruments measure the size, speed, direction, and force of the swirling clouds. The Hurricane Hunter radios its findings back to the Hurricane Center.

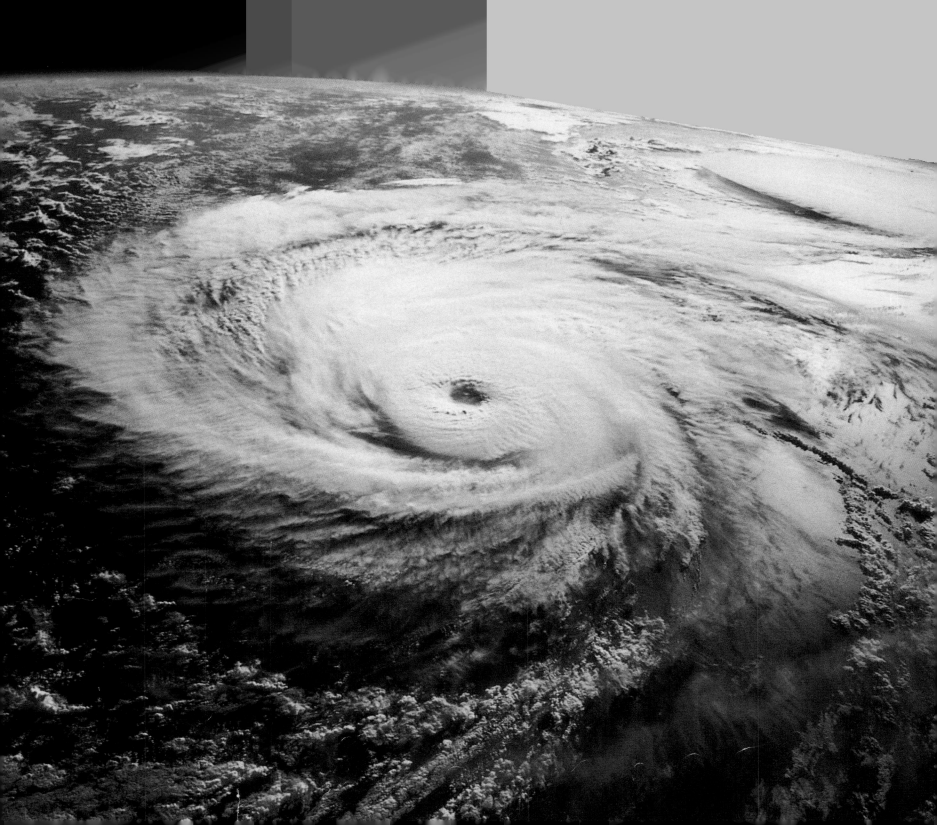

The meteorologists are alarmed by the report. Wind speeds have risen to over 100 miles per hour! They give Tropical Storm Andrew a new name. It is now known as Hurricane Andrew.

A *hurricane watch* is broadcast for the southeast coast. That means a hurricane has formed over the ocean and might reach the coast within two days.

Hurricanes are classified according to their wind speed. Category 1 hurricanes have winds of 74 to 95 miles per hour. That's enough to blow the leaves off the trees. The most powerful hurricanes are Category 5, with winds greater than 200 miles per hour—strong enough to tear up trees by their roots and bend lampposts to the ground.

Hurricanes usually form during the warmer months, when the sun heats the ocean surface, causing water to evaporate. As the warm water vapor rises, cooler air rushes in to replace it. Winds swirl around the rising column of moist air. When conditions are right, the rising water vapor condenses into clouds. The winds shape the clouds into an enormous white doughnut hundreds of miles across. The hole in the middle of a hurricane is called the *eye.* If you were in the eye of a hurricane, you could look straight up and see blue sky.

Hurricanes also occur over the Pacific and Indian Oceans. In this part of the world they are called *typhoons,* or tropical *cyclones.*

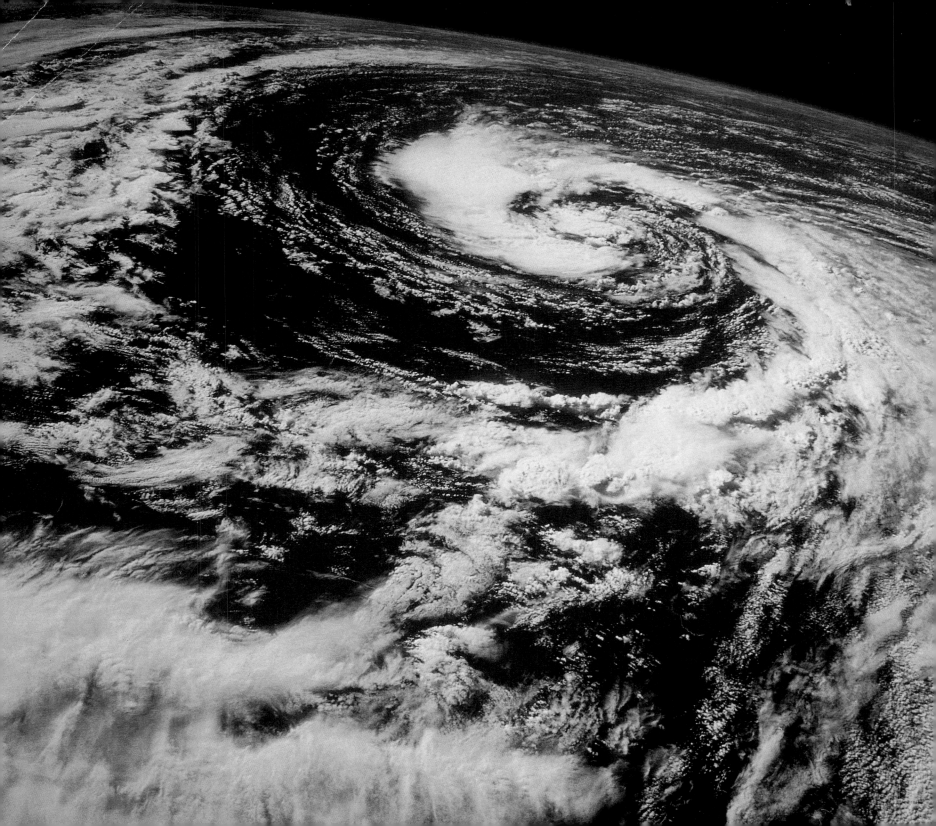

The giant, spinning storm known as Hurricane Andrew moves west. Will it reach the coast, or will it turn and head back out to sea? Computers calculate the path of the hurricane and try to figure out where it will go. Sometimes the computers are right. Other times, the hurricane seems to have a mind of its own!

As the storm gets closer, meteorologists use long-range radar to learn more. The hurricane grows in strength, with wind speeds of 150 miles per hour. According to the computers, Andrew will reach South Florida within 24 hours. The National Hurricane Center issues a *hurricane warning*.

When a hurricane warning is issued for your area, you should take it very seriously. Board up the windows. Bring your lawn furniture inside. If you live in a mobile home, you might want to strap your house to the earth with heavy cables. Most important, you should get in your car and drive inland to wait out the storm.

In 1958, scientists tried to slow down an approaching hurricane by dropping silver iodide crystals into the clouds. The experiment did not work. You can't stop a hurricane. When it comes to hurricanes, there is only one smart thing to do. Get out of its way!

You join the hundreds of thousands of people driving north, away from the storm. As you drive off, you look back at the ocean. Odd-looking clouds curve up from the horizon. They are *rooster tails*—the first sign of an approaching hurricane.

Soon, the sky grows dark and the rain begins to fall. The wind blows so hard the raindrops seem to be going sideways. Tree branches and roof shingles tumble through the air. The sewers back up, flooding the streets. A garbage can lid sails by like a giant Frisbee.

And that's only the beginning!

The worst hurricane damage is caused not by the wind and rain, but by the *storm surge*. As a hurricane nears land, the wind pushes a mound of water ahead of the storm, raising the level of the ocean as much as 20 feet. Imagine a wall of water as high as your house!

As Hurricane Andrew strikes the coast of Florida, the water rises. Buildings, trees, and animals are swept away. Homes and businesses that are not buried by the sea are torn apart by winds. Most of the people have fled. Of those who chose to stay, more than two dozen die.

The storm passes across the tip of Florida quickly, destroying 63,000 homes and causing 20 billion dollars in damage. But Andrew isn't finished yet! As the people of Florida return to their shattered homes, the hurricane continues its spinning journey across the Gulf of Mexico. Twenty-four hours later, Andrew crashes onto the coast of Louisiana, destroying more homes and businesses. From there, the storm moves inland, losing power as it leaves the warm waters of the Gulf. The winds slow down. By the time Andrew reaches northern Mississippi, it is just another rainstorm.

In 1900 a hurricane that hit Galveston, Texas, killed more than 6,000 people. Hurricane Andrew, a far worse hurricane, caused fewer than 65 deaths in 1992. The reason for the difference is that in 1900, there were no satellites, no weather planes, no radio, and no radar. People had no warning that a hurricane was about to strike. By the time they saw the rooster-tail clouds on the horizon, it was too late.

Today we still don't know how to stop a hurricane, but we know when one is on the way. And we know what to do.

Get out of its way!

INDEX

PHOTO RESEARCH
Kristee Flynn

PHOTO CREDITS
TONY STONE/NOAA: cover
TONY STONE/Kevin Kelley: 14
Warren Faidley/WEATHERSTOCK: 2, 24
SCIENCE PHOTO LIBRARY: 4
NASA/WEATHERSTOCK: 7
Carol Lee: 8
M. Laca/WEATHERSTOCK: 11
PHOTO RESEARCHERS/HaslerPierce, NASA: 13
PHOTO RESEARCHERS/Scott Camazine: 17
BRUCE COLEMAN/Norman Owen Tomalin: 18
D. Olsen/WEATHERSTOCK: 21
Herb Segars: 22
Tony Arruza: 27
WEATHERSTOCK: 28
PHOTONATS, INC./Laura C. Scheibel: 31

Library of Congress Cataloging-in-Publication Data
Murray, Peter, 1952 Sept. 29-
Hurricanes / by Peter Murray.
p. cm.
Includes Index.
ISBN 1-56766-196-3

1. Hurricanes--Juvenile literature.
2. Hurricanes–United States–Juvenile literature.
3. Hurricane Andrew, 1992–Juvenile literature.
[1. Hurricanes. 2. Hurricane Andrew, 1992.] I. Title.
QC944.2.M87   1995   95-1774
551.55'2--dc20

DATE DUE

FEB 07			
MAY 1 4			
SEP 2 2 1999